D0425658

Presented to

_____

From

_____

Date

_____

The Toddlers® Bedtime Story Book

The TODDLERS® Bedtime Story Book

V. Gilbert Beers

Illustrated by
Carole Boerke

VICTOR BOOKS

A DIVISION OF SCRIPTURE PRESS PUBLICATIONS INC.
USA CANADA ENGLAND

Published in Wheaton, Illinois by Victor Books/Scripture Press.

ISBN 1-56476-181-9

Printed in the United States of America
   3 4 5 6 7 – 99 98 97 96 95 94

Contents

Construction zone ahead...

You're about to enter one of the most important building projects of all time. It's bigger than the tunnel across the English Channel. It's bigger than the Empire State Building or the Golden Gate Bridge. It's bigger than constructing the ancient pyramids.

You're about to enter a life-building project with your child. It's BIG, even though he or she is so little, because so much is on the line.

Your toddler may look like a little kid. But one day your toddler's generation will manage the world. Your toddler will, in some way, have an important part in that management. Every world leader was once a toddler. Every world villain was once a toddler. During those toddler years, the leader or villain was under construction—with someone acting as general contractor. The end result of a lifetime of devout Christian service or villainous influence was the fruit of seeds sown during the toddler years.

More is accomplished during the first three years of life than any other three years. Think of the foundation stones laid—physical, mental, emotional, spiritual. These are the golden years of opportunity to build a life for Christ, and for the leadership role your toddler will have.

What is leadership? I think the key leadership role of all is that of parent. The others are important, but you, the parent, have the greatest opportunity of all to shape your child's life. You also have the greatest joy in doing it. In your role modeling as parent, you will cultivate in your toddler a strong sense of joy in parenting. Later your toddler will role model the delights of strong parenting to his or her child. What a delight that will be to you.

This is a unique book. It starts with the basic goal of joy or delight. I wanted to write stories that build that sense of joy or delight in toddlers as they listen and parents or teachers or friends as they read. It also enters into the heartbeat and mindset of the toddler. It is not written as a adult talking down to toddlers. They will NOT respond to that kind of writing. It must come from a writer who, while writing, has emptied himself or herself and becomes in heart and mind a toddler. That's what I have tried to do. It also presents real-life situations, and problems, that are common to toddlers. This is the stuff that you as a parent or teacher will recognize as the toddler's everyday experience.

Also this book seeks to acquaint the toddler with God and godliness, with values and the right way to live. It teams up with The Toddlers Bible to offer a life building program for your toddler. If you don't have a copy of The Toddlers Bible, be sure to get one and use it along with this book.

Why did I write this book? It was my delight to work in my home for 20 years when my 5 children were growing up. So I was able to interact with them many times each day. I have also had the delight of having my 8 grandchildren live nearby and we do special things together often. If that isn't enough, my daughter and her husband lived with us for 2 years when he was in seminary, and they had 2 beautiful little toddlers with whom Arlie and I could interact many times each day. We did! My Toddler Training Course has come from the laboratory of life with my 13 wonderful Toddlers and beyond over a period of almost 40 years.

I want to help you with life's biggest construction job of all—building the life of your VIP, the toddler God has entrusted into your care. I may not know your toddler, but I stopped just now to pray for him or her, that God will help you, and what I have done here, to shape that beautiful life forever.

—*V. Gilbert Beers*

I Want to See the Wind

"Where are you going?" Mother asked.
"I'm going to see the wind," said Jason.

Jason went outside. He felt the wind
blowing on his face. But he did not
see the wind.

Jason saw a kite. The wind was blowing
the kite. But Jason did not see the wind.

Jason blew some bubbles. The wind took the bubbles far away. But Jason did not see the wind.

A hat flew by. "Look at the hat go," said
Jason. The wind was blowing the hat. But
Jason did not see the wind.

The wind tugged at Jason's coat. Jason
tried to catch the wind. But he could not
catch it. He could not see it either.

Clouds raced across the sky. "The wind is blowing them," said Jason. He saw the clouds. But he did not see the wind.

Jason caught some wind in a jar. "Now I will see it," he said. But he could not see the wind.

"Did you see the wind?" Mother asked. "I saw the wind do many good things," said Jason. "But I did not see the wind."

"We can't see God either," said Mother.
"But we see Him do many good things."
"I'm glad He does many good things for
us," said Jason. "Thank You, God."

21

Look! What is the wind doing?

What is blowing with the wind?

Point to some of them.

You can see what
the wind is doing.

But can you see the
wind?

Why not?

Can you see God?
Why not?

A Piggy Room

"Look at the funny pigs," said Amy.
"Some are saying OINK," said Mommy.
"Some are rolling in the mud."

"They are so funny," said Amy. "They are messy too," said Mommy. "That pig pen looks like someone's room."

"MY room?" Amy asked. "Let's see," said Mommy. So Amy and Mommy went to Amy's room.

Look! This is Amy's room. What do you
see? This is what Amy saw. This is what
Mommy saw too.

"Oink!" said Amy. "I don't want a
piggy room. Will you help me?"

Amy picked up some toys. She put them on her shelves. Mommy helped her. Do you think they are having fun?

Amy picked up her clothes. She hung
them in her closet. You can see Mommy
helping her, can't you?

Amy also picked up her stuffed animals.
Do you see what she is doing with them?

"Thank you for helping me, Mommy,"
said Amy. "My piggy room is now a
pretty room."

"Let's thank God for your pretty room,"
said Mommy. Do you think they did?

What is Amy doing in her room?

Who is helping her?

Point to some things they are doing together.

Why is Amy cleaning her room?

Why is Mommy
helping her?

Is your room clean
or messy?

What should you do
about it?

Who Could Make These Things?

Who could make a puffy cloud
away up in the sky?

Who could make the apples in
Mommy's apple pie?

Who could make that woolly worm
That squiggle-wiggled by?

Who could make the tallest tree
That reaches up so high?

Who could make that flying thing
That's called a butterfly?

Who could make a baby
That can coo or laugh or cry?

Who could make the twinkle
In my Mommy's twinkly eye?

I cannot make these special things,
And I really don't know why.

But since I know what God can do,

I will not even try!

Do you see a woolly worm?

Do you see some tall trees?

Point to some butterflies.

Point to a baby.

Who made all
these things?

Have you thanked
Him?

Will you do that
now?

Grow Seeds Grow

"Let's plant some flower seeds," said
Daddy. He took a shovel and rake to the
back yard. He took some flower seeds too.

Daddy dug the dirt. He moved the rake
back and forth. Soon the dirt was soft.

"Now I need some helpers," said Daddy.
So Jory and Jerry helped Daddy put seeds
in the dirt.

"Now they will grow to be beautiful flowers," said Daddy.

Jory and Jerry sat down by the dirt.
They looked at the dirt.

"What are you doing?" Daddy asked.
"Watching flowers grow," said Jory.
"Now!" said Jerry.

Daddy smiled. "We can't see them grow today," he said. "First the sun must smile at the seeds. A few drops of rain will help too."

"The seeds will feel the sun and rain,"
said Daddy. "Little green plants will
come from the seeds. The flowers will
grow on the plants. But we must wait."

"We will come here each day," said
Daddy. "One day you will see the green
plants. Later you will see the flowers."

Each day Jory and Jerry watched the
plants grow. One day they saw beautiful
flowers. They took some to Mommy. "I'm
glad we waited," they said. "So am I,"
said Mommy. "Thank you!"

What is Daddy planting?

Who is helping him?

What will help the seeds grow?

What grew from the seeds?

Who helps seeds
grow?
Have you thanked
God for doing this?

Thank You, God

Thank You, God, for my hands,
so I can clap them when I'm happy

Thank You, God, for my arms,
so I can hug my Mommy and Daddy.

Thank You, God, for my eyes,
so I can see my Mommy and Daddy.

Thank You, God, for my ears,
so I can hear stories about You.

Thank You, God, for my feet,
so I can walk to church.

Thank You, God, for my lips,
so I can sing songs about You.

Thank You, God, for my legs,
so I can run and play.

Thank You, God, for my fingers,
so I can touch my kitty's fur.

Thank You, God, for my mouth,
so I can eat Your good food.

Thank You, God, for making me, so
I can love Mommy, Daddy, and You.

Who made your feet?
What can your feet do?
Who made your lips?
What can your lips do?
Who made your eyes
and ears?

What can they help you do?

What else did God make for you?

Will you thank Him now?

He Did It!

Do you see what Gloria is doing? What do you think will happen?

Look at that mess! And look at poor little
Gary. Gloria is running away. She does not
want Mommy to think that she did this.

"Oh, Gary, what have you done?"
Mommy cries out. Gloria is glad Mommy
thinks he did it. So Gloria says nothing.

"You must not do that, Gary," Mommy says. She mops up the spilled juice. But Gloria still says nothing.

Gary is crying. Gloria feels sad. But now she is afraid to tell Mommy.

Gloria is hiding behind a chair. She wants to cry. She has not really lied to Mommy. But she has not told Mommy the truth either.

Now Gloria knows what she must do.
She is running to Mommy. She is crying.
Gloria will tell Mommy what really
happened.

"I didn't lie to you," says Gloria. "But I
didn't tell the truth. I guess that is like
lying. I'm sorry."

"What do you want to say to Gary?"
Mommy asks. So Gloria says, "I'm sorry,"
to Gary too. Then she hugs him.

Do you think Gloria's family is happy now?

Do you see a mess?
Point to it.
Who made the mess?
Why did Gloria cry?

82

What did Gloria tell Mommy?
Why did this make her happy?

Pass the Rolls

"I want the rolls," said Brendon. Mommy and Daddy did not pass the rolls. "How should you ask?" said Mommy.

"Pass the rolls," said Brendon. Mommy
and Daddy did not pass the rolls. "How
should you ask?" said Daddy.

"I want the rolls," said Brendon. Mommy and Daddy were quiet. They did not pass the rolls. "Aren't you forgetting something?" Mommy asked.

Brendon began to whine. "Rolls!" said
Brendon. But Mommy and Daddy did
not pass the rolls. "What should you
say?" said Daddy.

"Why can't you pass the rolls?" said
Brendon. "I've asked and asked!" But
Mommy and Daddy did not pass the rolls.

"Did you hear someone ask for rolls?"
Mommy said to Daddy. "I hear better
when someone says PLEASE," said
Daddy.

"Please pass the rolls," said Mommy. "I'll be happy to," said Daddy. He passed the rolls to her.

"Please pass the rolls back to me," said
Daddy. "I'll be happy to," said Mommy.
She passed the rolls to Daddy.

"Please pass the rolls," said Brendon. "I'll be happy to," said Daddy. He passed the rolls to Brendon.

"Please remember to say please," said
Daddy. "I'll be happy to," said Brendon.
Do you think he remembered?

What does Brendon want?

How is he asking for the rolls?

How should he ask?

What magic word
did he forget?
Can you say please?
Will you remember
to say please today?

Shhhh! Daddy Is Praying

Shhhh, table.
Daddy is praying.
He is thanking God for our good dinner.

Shhhh, chair.
Daddy is praying.
He is thanking God for Mommy

Shhhh, big brother.
Daddy is praying.
He is thanking God for you.

Shhhh, kitty.
Daddy is praying.
He is thanking God for church.

Shhhh, puppy.
Daddy is praying.
He is thanking God for our Bible.

Shhhh, door. Daddy is praying.
He is thanking God that we can play
together.

Shhhh, bed. Daddy is praying.
He is thanking God for warm beds where
we can sleep tonight.

Shhhh, jeans. Daddy is praying.
He is thanking God for our good clothes.

Shhhh, me. Daddy is praying.
He is thanking God that we love each
other.

Shhhhhh. Daddy has stopped praying.
Now it's my turn.
Is it your turn, too?

Shhh!
But why should you shhh?
What is Daddy doing?

Shhh!
Who is Daddy talking to?
Would you like to talk to God too?

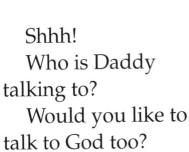

Danny's Candy Bar

Mommy paid for the groceries. She picked up the grocery bags. Danny walked behind her.

Then Danny saw a candy bar. He wanted it. So Danny picked it up. He put it in his pocket.

Danny felt sad all the way home. He knew that he had done something wrong.

"You're so quiet, Danny," said Mommy.
"Is something wrong?" Danny turned
away from Mommy. He did not want to
look at her.

"Something IS wrong," said Mommy.
"Please tell me so I can help you." Then
Danny showed Mommy the candy bar.

"Oh, Danny, did you get this at the grocery store?" Mommy asked. Danny looked at Mommy sadly. "Yes," he said.

"Then we must go back to the store,"
said Mommy. "You must give this
back to the man there."

"I'm sorry," Danny said to the man.
The man smiled.

"Would you like me to buy the candy bar
for you?" Mommy asked Danny.
"Please," said Danny.

"I'm sorry you took the candy," Mommy
told Danny. "But I'm glad you told me
the truth. Thank you." Then Danny
shared his candy bar with Mommy.

What did Danny do
that he should not do?
Why was he sad?

What did Danny say
to the man at the store?
Why is he happy
now?

Sharing a Sandwich

Alan and Allison are having a picnic.
Alan has a big sandwich. But Allison
forgot to bring a sandwich.

"Why don't you eat your sandwich?" Alan asked. "Because I don't have a sandwich," said Allison.

Alan picked up his big sandwich. He almost took a bite. But he saw Allison watching him. Allison looked hungry.

"Please take my sandwich," said Alan.
So he gave his sandwich to Allison.

Allison picked up Alan's big sandwich.
She almost took a bite. But she saw Alan
watching her. Alan looked hungry.

"I can't eat this," said Allison. "You don't have a sandwich. What will we do?"

Alan and Allison looked at the sandwich. They were very sad. Each wanted the other to have something to eat. But each was hungry.

Then Allison had an idea. "Why don't we share the sandwich?" she asked. She gave half to Alan. She kept half for herself.

Now look how happy they both are. Alan
has half of the sandwich. Allison has half
of the sandwich. Each has the same to eat.

"It's fun to share," said Alan. "Sharing makes us BOTH happy," said Allison. Do you think they are? Are you happy when you share?

Who forgot a sandwich?
Who brought a sandwich?
Who ate the sandwich?

Do you like to share?

What do you share with others?

Why do you share?

131

Will You Be My Friend?

"Will you be my friend?" Kevin asked.
But the stuffed lion said nothing.

"Will you be my friend?" Kevin asked.
But the picture near his bed said nothing.

"Will you be my friend?" Kevin asked.
The snowman outside almost looked as
if he could talk. But he didn't.

"Will you be my friend?" Kevin asked.
The little sparrow at the bird feeder
looked at Kevin. Then it flew away.

"Will you be my friend?" Kevin asked.
But the cloud in the sky kept on going.

"Will you be my friend?" Kevin asked.
The little tree bowed with the wind. But
it said nothing.

"Will you be my friend?" Kevin asked. The squirrel stopped and looked at Kevin. Then he hurried up the tree with his acorn.

"No one will be my friend," said Kevin.
He sat down on a big stump. He was sad.

"I'll be your friend," said a voice.
Kevin turned to see who it was.
"Daddy!" he shouted. Then he ran
to give Daddy a big hug.

"Mommy and I are your almost very best friends," said Daddy. "But who is my very best friend?" asked Kevin. Do you think it is God?

Kevin wanted a friend.
Who did he ask?
Point to each of them.

Who were Kevin's almost best friends?
Who was Kevin's really best friend?

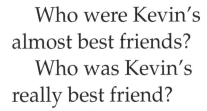

Thank You, Mommy

Thank you, Mommy, for waking up my day. Thank you for your smile that says "good morning!"

Thank you, Mommy, for helping me get dressed. Thank you for washing and ironing my clothes for me.

Thank you, Mommy, for that yummy smell of breakfast. Thank you for saying, "I love you" by giving me good food to eat.

Thank you, Mommy, for playing with me.
Thank you for that last big push that
made me go so high.

Thank you, Mommy, for hugs when I cry.
Thank you for kissing my "owie" when I
hurt my finger.

Thank you, Mommy, for a happy house
where I can play. Thank you for helping
me keep it so nice and clean.

Thank you, Mommy, for hugging Daddy when he comes home. Thank you for telling Daddy and me, "I love you."

Thank you, Mommy, for my toys and things around my room. Thank you for helping me pick them up and put them where I should.

Thank you, Mommy, for storytime.
Thank you for loving me enough to read
each night to me.

Thank you, Mommy, for tucking me into bed. Thank you for being there so I can say, "Good night."

Thank you, Mommy,
the girl said.
What for?
Point to each

picture. Tell the story to
your Mommy.

Then say, Thank you
to her.

Thunder and Lightning

"Mommy, I'm afraid," said Eric. "The thunder and lightning are so scary."
"It's OK," said Mommy. "God sends the thunder and lightning."

"But why?" asked Eric. "Perhaps He knows you need some Mommy hugs," said Mommy. "Perhaps He knows you need the rain that comes too."

"But why does God send rain?" asked Eric.
"Why can't we always have sunshine?"

"God sends water so the plants will grow," said Mommy. "But why?" asked Eric.

"Some plants give you peas or corn or beans," said Mommy. Eric rubbed his tummy. "Some give you strawberries." "I like strawberries," said Eric.

"God sends the rain so grass can grow," said Mommy. "Cows eat grass and give you good milk."

"God sends the rain so flowers can grow," said Mommy. "You like to smell the wonderful flowers, don't you?" Of course Eric said yes.

"God sends rain so we can have trees and bushes too," said Mommy. "You can hear the wind whisper in their leaves."

"I'm not afraid of thunder and lightning now," said Eric. "I'm glad God sends rain. Thank You, God."

"Good night, Mommy," said Eric.
"Good night, God."

What made Eric afraid?

Are you ever afraid?

Why?

What did Eric's
Mommy say to him.
Why does God send
lightning and thunder?
You're not afraid
now, are you?

Mine!

"Mine!" said Tammy. "No, mine!" said Tommy. Mommy frowned. "OK," she said. "Who had it first?"

"I did," said Tammy. "No, I did," said
Tommy.

"But I was first," said Tammy. "No, I was first," said Tommy. Then they began to argue.

Mommy took the teddy bear. "Let's play with teddy bear later," she said. "I have some cookies in the kitchen."

Tammy and Tommy were excited when
they saw the cookies Mommy had made.
"Yummy!" they shouted.

"They're MINE!" said Mommy. "You can't have any." Tammy and Tommy looked surprised. But they remembered how they had said "mine."

173

"But. . . but I just want one," said Tammy.
"Me too," said Tommy. "No," said
Mommy. "I had them first."

Tammy and Tommy remembered how
they had said, "I was first." Now they
were sorry they had said it. Tammy ran to
get teddy.

"Yours," said Tammy. "You had Teddy first." "Let's play with Teddy together," said Tommy. "That's much more fun."

"And let's share the cookies," said
Mommy. "That's much more fun too." So
they did! The next time you say "MINE"
think of Tammy and Tommy.

Who said "Mine!"
What did Mommy do?

Do you ever say "Mine?"

You won't now, will you?

179

Thank You, God, for Water

Thank You, God, for water. Thank You
for a cool drink on a hot summer day.

Thank You, God, for water. Thank You for ice cubes that make my cool drink colder.

Thank You, God, for water. I couldn't swim in my little pool without water.

Thank You, God, for water. Our flowers
are glad that they can have a drink too.

Thank You, God, for water. Our family
couldn't do this without water, could we?

Thank You, God, for water. Thank You for a gentle rain that helps our garden grow.

Thank You, God, for water. Thank You
that we can wash our dirty dishes. It
wouldn't be fun to eat from dirty dishes.

Thank You, God, for water. Thank You for water where my goldfish can swim.

Thank You, God, for water. Thank You for a warm bath. My duckie thanks You, too.

Thank You, God, for water. Thank You for saying, "I love you" by giving me water for all these things.

Look at the pictures.
How is water used
in each one?

Who gives us our water?
What should we say to God?

Whine-itis

"Mommeee!" Rachel whined. "This sock won't go on." Rachel was whining. Do you ever do that?

"Mommeee!" Rachel whined again.
"I can't find my shoes." What was Rachel
doing?

"Is my little Rachel OK?" Mommy asked.
Mommy put her hand on Rachel's face.

"Am I sick?" Rachel asked.

"I think you have a little whine-itis,"
said Mommy. "It's like being sick when
you're not really sick."

"What's whine-itis?" asked Rachel.
"It's when little girls or boys whine
too much," said Mommy.

"But how can I get well from whine-itis?" asked Rachel.

"Stop whining," said Mommy. "If you don't, I may catch it. Then I'll start whining. You wouldn't want that, would you?"

Rachel giggled. "You're teasing me,
aren't you, Mommy?" she said. "But
I'll stop. Every time I start to whine,
I'll think of whine-itis."

So that's what happened. Every time Rachel started to whine, she thought of whine-itis. Then she stopped. Will you do that too?

Why did Rachel whine?

What did Mommy call this?

202

How did Mommy
help Rachel stop
whining?

If you whine
sometime, will you
remember Rachel?

Sweet, Sour, Hot and Cold

"Ummm," said Katy. "This ice cream tastes good." "How do you know it tastes good?" Mommy asked. Katy looked surprised.

"Your taster tells you that," said Mommy. "What else does a taster tell me?" asked Katy.

"Taste this," said Mommy. She held a little pickle for Katy. "Ohhh, that's SOUR," said Katy. "My ice cream cone is SWEET."

"How about this chocolate in my cup?"
Mommy asked. Katy took a sip. "It's HOT,"
she said. "My ice cream cone is COLD."

"Your taster also tells you it is
CHOCOLATE," said Mommy. "And it tells
you that your ice cream is VANILLA."

"Lick your finger and try this," said
Mommy. She shook some salt into her
hand. Katy tasted it. "It's SALTY," she said.

"Your taster knows when you're eating PEPPERMINT, PEACH, APPLE or ORANGE," said Mommy. "It's a wonderful taster!"

"Where did I get such a wonderful
taster?" asked Katy.

"God gave it to you," said Mommy.

"Thank You, God," said Katy. Have you
thanked God today for your taster?

What did Katy taste?
Have you tasted
something special
today?
What was it?

Who gave you your taster?

Will you say "Thank You, God?"

Listen! What Do You Hear?

Listen! What do you hear? I hear my kitty purring. She says, "I love you."

Listen! What do you hear? I hear the wind.
It is sighing in the tree. I think it is
whispering something to me.

Listen! What do you hear? Puppy is
barking. He wants to play with me.
"Thank you, Puppy, for wanting to play."

Listen! What do you hear? A fire engine is
going by. The firemen will help someone.
I'm glad for firemen who help us.

Listen! What do you hear? The doorbell is ringing. Oh, look! There is my friend. We will play together.

Listen! What do you hear? A bird is
singing. It is saying, "Good morning!
Time to get up!"

Listen! What do you hear? Big sister is
playing the piano. I like to hear her play.
Sometimes she lets me help her.

Listen! What do you hear? Daddy is whispering to Mommy. I think he is saying, "I love you." I hope so. That makes me glad.

Listen! What do you hear? Mommy
is reading a story to me. "Thank you,
Mommy. I love you."

Listen! What do you hear? I hear many
wonderful sounds. God made each one for
me. "Thank You, God. I love You too."

Listen! What do you hear now?

What did the boys and girls in the story hear?

Listen! Who made the sounds that you hear?

Thank God for each one now.

Let's Eat!

"Let's eat!" said Joshua. He started
to open the picnic basket.

"Wait!" said Daddy. "I think
we have forgotten something."

Joshua looked around. There was the blanket. There was the picnic basket. There were Mommy and Daddy. And there was Joshua.

"What did we forget?" asked Joshua.
"We forgot to DO something special,"
said Daddy.

"Mommy put the food in the basket," said Joshua. "Daddy drove us out here. And we all spread out the blanket."

"We forgot to thank someone,"
said Daddy.

"Thank you, Mommy, for making the picnic lunch," said Joshua.

"Thank you, Daddy, for bringing us here," said Joshua.

"And thank You, God, for giving us this wonderful picnic," Daddy prayed.

"Oh, we must remember to thank God," said Joshua. "Yes, we must," said Daddy. "And we did! Now we may eat." So they did.

What is this family doing?

Who did Joshua thank?

Why did he thank each one?

Why did Daddy thank God?

Why should you thank God for your food?

Thank You for My House

Thank You, God, for my house. Thank You for the kitchen. Mommy makes wonderful food for me there.

Thank You, God, for my house.
Thank You for the back door. That's
where I run outside to play.

Thank You, God, for my house. Thank You for our washing machine. That helps me have clean clothes to wear.

Thank You, God, for my house. Thank
You for my bedroom. It's so warm and
cozy. I love to play there too.

Thank You, God, for my house. Thank You for the chair where Daddy sits. He likes to read to me there.

Thank You, God, for my house. Thank You for the stairs. It's so much fun to walk to my room. It's fun to bump down the stairs, too.

Thank You, God, for my house. Thank You that it's nice and warm on a cold winter night.

Thank You, God, for my house. Thank You for the bathroom. Mommy helps me get fresh and clean there.

Thank You, God, for my house. Thank You for my closet. I'm glad when Mommy helps me hang up my clothes.

Thank You, God, for my house. Thank
You for all of it. I know You helped
Mommy and Daddy get it. Thank You.
Thank You.

Look at each picture. Each one is a "thank you" picture. Why?

Who gave us our houses?

Why should we thank Him?

251

Surprises

Do you like surprises? Jonathan does.
"That's why I like to open birthday
presents," says Jonathan.

Jonathan likes to hide. Christopher tries to find him. Surprise! There's Jonathan.

Christopher likes surprises too. "Watch when I break this egg shell," says Mommy. No one has even seen that egg before.

"Guess what we're having for dinner
tonight?" Mommy asks. No one knows.
Surprise! Look at that!

"Guess who's behind you," says
Jonathan. Christopher pretends that he
doesn't know. "Surprise!" says Jonathan.

"Look at this, Jonathan," says Daddy. "No one has ever seen the nut inside." Daddy cracks the shell. Out comes a nut.

"Please open the door," says Mommy.
Jonathan and Christopher open the door.
"Happy birthday!" their friends sing.
"Surprise!"

"Surprise, Christopher; surprise,
Jonathan," says Mommy. "It's a brand
new day. Time to get up."

"Surprise!" says Mommy again. "I'm going to read something from this brand new book."

"Surprise! I love you, Mommy," says Christopher. "Surprise! I love you too," says Jonathan.

What surprises do you see?

Which do you like best?

Have you surprised Mommy or Daddy with "I love you?"

Would you like to now?

Good Morning

Good morning, sunshine. Thank you for coming through my window.

Good morning, room. Thank you that
you are MY room.

Good morning, Teddy Bear. Thank you for staying with me last night.

Good morning, kitty. Thank you for kissing me. Are you saying "good morning" to me too?

Good morning, Mommy. Thank you for
being MY Mommy. I love you.

Good morning, toothbrush. Thank you for scrubbing that funny taste from my mouth.

Good morning, clothes. Thank you for being my friends today.

Good morning, breakfast. Thank you that
you wake up my tummy.

Good morning, world. Thank you for
being a beautiful world.

Good morning, God.
Thank You for everything I have.
You are a wonderful God.

Good morning!
Would you like to say
that to something?
Would you like to
say it to someone?
Who?

Did you say "Good morning" to God this morning?

Would you like to now?

I'm Glad I'm Not a Turtle

I'm glad I'm not a turtle;
I'm glad I'm not a frog.

I'm glad I'm not a puppy,
Or a giant hairy dog.

I'm glad I'm not an elephant
That lives inside the zoo.

I'm glad I'm not that jumpy thing
That's called a kangaroo.

I'm glad I'm not a bunny
With long ears and twitchy nose.

I'm glad I'm not a nanny goat
With funny looking toes.

I'm glad I'm not this little guy,
I know that you are too.

I'm glad that I am who I am,
I'm glad that you are you.

I'm glad that God made us
In His very special way.

And I'm glad that I can thank Him
On this very special day.

Are you glad you're not a frog, or a hairy dog, or a kangaroo?

Are you glad God made you the way you are?

Would you like to thank Him now?

I'm Coming!

"Andrea, will you please come here?"
Mommy called. "I'm coming," said
Andrea. But she kept on playing with
her doll.

"Andrea, I'm waiting for you," Mommy called. "In a minute," Andrea called back. But she was petting her kitty now.

"Are you coming, Andrea?" Mommy
called. "Yes," said Andrea. But she
wasn't. She was drawing now.

"I'm waiting, Andrea,"
said Mommy. "Be right there," said
Andrea. But she was looking at a book.

"Andrea?" said Mommy. "Coming!" said
Andrea. But she was watching some
children play outside.

"Anyone home?" said Mommy. "I'm almost there," said Andrea. But she was lying on the floor cuddling her blanket.

"Last call," said Mommy. This time
Andrea did not even answer.

Andrea did not hear Mommy call again. Before long she wondered what Mommy wanted. So she ran to the kitchen.

"Did you call, Mommy?" Andrea asked.
"I thought you might like to lick your
favorite chocolate from the beaters," said
Mommy. "Oh, yes!" said Andrea.

"But you're too late," said Mommy. "Last call was really the last call. I had to wash them." Do you think Andrea came the next time Mommy called?

What is Andrea doing?

What should Andrea be doing?

What did Mommy want her to do?

What should you do when Mommy calls for you?

My Shadow and I

My shadow and I went for a walk.

I ran. My shadow ran too. "I'll go this way," I said. "You go that way." But my shadow would not obey me.

I waved my arms. My shadow waved its arms too. "Stop doing that!" I said. But my shadow would not obey me.

When I jumped, my shadow jumped as high as I did. "Stop jumping!" I said. My shadow did not listen to me.

"Stop doing everything I do, shadow," I said. Do you think my shadow obeyed me?

"Go away shadow!" I shouted.
Why doesn't my shadow obey me?

"Will you please obey me shadow?" I said.
But my shadow won't even answer me.

Didn't Mommy say that to me this morning? Didn't she say, "Will you please obey me?"

I guess Mommy doesn't like it when I don't obey her. I'm sorry, Mommy.

Maybe God doesn't like it when I don't obey Him. I'm sorry, God.

What did the
shadow do?
Why didn't it obey?
What did the boy
think about that?

What does Mommy think when you do not obey?

What does God think when you do not obey?

Where Did Tina Go?

"Where did Tina go?" Mommy asked.
"And listen to this grouchy lion." "I can't
find my socks!" the lion growls.

"Where did Tina go?" Mommy asked.
"And listen to this thumpy elephant."
Tina would not jump and thump like that.

"Where did Tina go?" Mommy asked.
"And where did this messy piggy come
from?" Look at the way that piggy eats.

"Where did Tina go?" Mommy asked. "And where did this scarecrow come from?" Tina never looks that messy, does she?

"Where did Tina go?" Mommy asked. "I asked her to hurry. But look at this turtle. It is so slow."

"Where did Tina go?" Mommy asked.
"It's time for her bath. And where did
this splashy duck come from?"

"Where did Tina go?" Mommy asked.
"Listen to this big doggy howl." "I don't
want to go to bed," the hairy dog howls.

"Where did Tina go?" Mommy asked.
"Oh, there she is!"

"I'm glad my Tina is here," said Mommy.
"Those animals were strange. They wouldn't
help me keep things neat and clean."

"I'll be your helper," said Tina. "I told all those strange animals to go away. I will help you keep things neat and clean."

Tina was like some animals.

What kind? How was she like them?

Are you ever like these animals?

Does your Mommy like that?

Who does she want you to be?

Who does God want you to be?

I'm Not a Robin

Today I saw a robin fly. I tried to fly too.
But you can see what happened. How
do you do that, robin?

Today I saw a bunny hop. I tried to hop too. I guess the bunny does it better than I can.

Today I heard my puppy bark. I tried to bark too. It was so silly!

Today I heard my kitty purr. I tried to
purr too. Have you ever done that?

Today I saw a horse gallop. I tried to gallop too. I wouldn't make a very good horse, would I?

Today I saw a frog jump. I tried to jump like a frog. Frogs jump much better!

Today I saw a squirrel climb a tree.
I tried, but I couldn't do that. How
do you do it, squirrel?

Today I heard a rooster crow. Can you crow like a rooster? I tried. But I can't do it.

Today I tried to be a boy. Do you
know what? I can do all the things
a boy or girl should.

Thank You, God! I'm glad
You made me the way I am.

Are you a robin or a bunny?

Can you fly like a bird?

Look at each animal or bird.

Who made them that way?

Look in the mirror.

Who made you the way you are?

Will you thank Him now?

335

Bedtime

"I don't want to go to bed," said Sarah.
"I want to stay up all night."

"But you will get tired and wiggly," said
Mommy. "You need your sleep."

"I'm a big girl now," said Sarah.
"Big girls don't need to go to bed."

"All right," said Mommy. "Let's
see what happens. Good night."

Mother went to her chair to read.
Sarah began to look at her books.
Suddenly she yawned.

"I am NOT sleepy," Sarah said to herself. "I am a big girl. I will NOT go to bed." Then Sarah played with her stuffed animals.

341

Sarah played with toys. She looked at more books. She played with stuffed animals. Then Sarah yawned a BIG yawn.

Sarah wiggled. She squirmed. She rolled
on the floor. She was SO tired. She almost
wanted to cry.

Sarah ran to Mommy's chair. She climbed
into Mommy's arms. Then she yawned the
BIGGEST yawn of all. "Sleepy?" Mother
asked.

Mommy carried Sarah to her room. She tucked her into bed. "Good night," said Mommy. But Sarah did not say a word. She was asleep. Are you sleepy too?

Where is Sarah's bed?

Where is Sarah?

Why isn't she sleeping?

Do you like bedtime?

Say, "Thank You, God, for sleep."

Good night!

Values Taught

in The Toddlers Bedtime Story Book